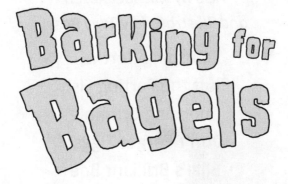

Barking for Bagels

Also by Michael Rosen
and illustrated by Tony Ross:

Burping Bertha
Fluff the Farting Fish
Choosing Crumble
Don't Forget Tiggs!
Bilal's Brilliant Bee
Hampstead the Hamster

Barking for Bagels

MICHAEL ROSEN

ILLUSTRATED BY TONY ROSS

Andersen Press
London

First published in 2017 by
Andersen Press Limited
20 Vauxhall Bridge Road
London SW1V 2SA
www.andersenpress.co.uk

4 6 8 10 9 7 5 3

British Library Cataloguing in Publication Data available.

ISBN 978 1 78344 505 9

Printed and bound in India

Chapter One

My name is Shnipp.

I am a dog.

This is my story.

A dog's story.

Shnipp's story.

It is the truth, the whole truth and nothing but the truth.

By the way:

this is my tooth, the whole tooth and nothing but the tooth . . .

I used to be looked after by Julie and Lara and their mum, Sadie.

Am I still looked after by Julie and Lara
and Sadie?

Aha!

I may be.

I may not be.

You won't know if I am or I am not till
you get to the end of the story.

If this was a film, you would now hear "der der der der-der" music. But it's not a film, it's a book, so there's no music. Sorry.

One day, Julie and Lara and Sadie took me to the park. The Memorial Park. We were playing the throw, fetch, leave game with a ball.

"Cooeee! Shnipp!" they called.

It was great. I was doing some great running, really fast. A couple of times I actually caught the ball in mid-air. You know when the ball comes flying through the air? I caught it in my mouth before it dropped!

Skills!

"Cooeee! Shnipp!" they called.

Anyway, just as I was thinking how good I am, another thought popped into my head. I thought, *Hey, what if I go for a big run? You know, just run off?*

And . . . if I did happen to run off, I would never ever have to hear Julie and Lara snickering ever again.

Snickering.

What is snickering?

Snickering is the noise that Julie and Lara make when they laugh. It sounds a bit like they are sneezing backwards, over and over again.

Look, don't get me wrong here. I loved
Julie and Lara. I loved them very, very,
very, very, very much. I loved running
round and round the back yard with
them. I loved the way they called out
"Cooeee! Shnipp!" But I didn't like the
snickering.

Anyway, I was thinking all this, and I just started running. Running away from Julie and Lara and Sadie. I just went for it.

You might like to make that noise:

Vrooo o o o o sh!

Well, I kept on running, kept on running, kept on running until I got to some woods. That felt great. I ran through some bushes and the bushes brushed up against me and it felt like someone was brushing my coat.

Just then I noticed a fox.

You never know when you might meet a fox if you're out and about.

And I was most certainly, absolutely and totally "out and about".

Now, I've got nothing against foxes. I really haven't. Foxes do their thing, I do mine.

Here are my thoughts about foxes.

Foxes really like rubbish. You know, when people leave out bags of rubbish in the street, they love that. They spend hours and hours going through it. I once saw a fox eating eggshells. What? Eggshells? What is the matter with them?

Another one I saw was eating a newspaper. I'm not joking: eating a newspaper. Do you eat newspapers? I don't think so. Neither do I.

I don't mean to sound like a snob.
I don't mean to look down my nose at
them – OK, yes, I do have a big nose but
that's what dogs have.

Anyway, foxes eat rubbish. That's the
way they are. I don't. Though I have to
admit, foxes are very funny. They're very
good at jokes. Especially "knock knock"
jokes.

So the fox came up to me and told me
a "knock knock" joke:

I think that's really, really, really funny.

Perhaps you don't.

I said, "Hey, that's really funny."

And he said, "Glad you like it, Shnipp. Stay lucky."

I said, "How do you know my name?"
But he was off and away.
No answer.

That's what foxes are like.

And that's the end of my thoughts about foxes.

Anyway, I came out of the woods and thought that maybe I should go home now, but to tell you the truth, I didn't know where I was.

Chapter Two

Yes, I was lost.

But I just carried on running. I'm rather good at running. It's a dog thing. Run, run, run. On, on, on. I ran until I got to a market. It was a place where they were selling cooked food.

And oh my, oh my, oh my, oh my, the smell . . .

Oh, the smell.

Oh, the *smell*.

The lovely, lovely smell.

I'll just have to stop telling this story for a moment while I think about that lovely, lovely, lovely smell.

Oh my, oh my, oh my, oh my, the smell.
(I'm still thinking about it.)

You have no idea just how gorgeous and juicy and utterly sumptuous this smell was. I just had to stop and smell it all in.

Yes, I stood there. Breathing in all the smells. And I have a truly amazing nose, you know. (Have I mentioned my nose already?) With my nose, I could smell all the different smells from all the different stalls and vans.

Over on one side there was some Moroccan chicken.

On the other there were prime beef hamburgers.

Along the road a bit there was some paella. You might think that a dog wouldn't like fish and seafood. Oh no, I love it.

There were some fantastic salad dishes. I love salad, me. Oh yes.

And bagels. Oh, fresh, warm, soft, chewy bagels.

I can tell you, I was barking for those bagels.

Now, you're not going to believe this, but I strolled up to the bagel van and stood there. OK, maybe my face was looking a bit begging-ish, if you get me. You know, a bit pleading. A bit naggy. And the woman on the van, do you know what she did? She threw me a bagel.

Oh, that bagel. That was the nicest, loveliest, softest, sweetest, most fantastic bagel in the universe.

And once I had tasted that bagel, I never wanted to eat anything else ever again. I never wanted to be with anyone else other than Bessie the Bagel Lady who gave me the bagel.

So I stood by Bessie's Bagel Van all that morning and all that lunchtime, until she started to wrap up all her stuff. Then, just when her back was turned and she was about to close the back door of her van, I jumped in and hid under a cupboard inside.

And after a few minutes, off went
Bessie's Bagel Van with me in it.

And I stayed for a while with Bessie the Bagel Lady and it was very nice. She was nice to me. I was nice to her. And I ate bagels.

Though I have to say, because I was eating bagels every day . . .

and all day . . .

. . . I was starting to put on weight.

Now I know what you're thinking.

You're thinking, *How awful. What about Julie and Lara and Sadie? Weren't they upset?*

I'm going to be honest.

At the time, I didn't know if they were upset and I wasn't thinking about it. Call me bad, call me naughty if you like, but it's true.

I'm sorry. But that's the truth, the whole truth and nothing but the truth.

Then one day I was out in the Bagel Van and I heard the foxes outside.

They knew I was in the van. And they called out to me.

"Shnipp! Shnipp!"

"Yes?" I said.

"Julie and Lara and Sadie are out looking for you. They're calling 'Cooeee! Shnipp!' for you everywhere. They're looking for you everywhere. They've put up notices everywhere."

"Notices?" I said. "What do they say?"

So they told me about the poster.

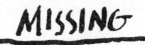

MISSING

Our gorgeous, loveliest black-and-white family dog called "Shnipp".

We love her so so so so so so much and we miss her lots and lots and lots.

If you see her, here she is:

please ring us: 0555555 676767

"Oh," I said.

"And something else," they said.

"What?" I said.

"They've left the door to the back yard open for you so that if you ever come past, you can just drop in," said one of the foxes.

"Anyway," said another, "stay lucky."

And off they went.

I went back to sit in the van and think.

Julie and Lara and Sadie did all that just for me.

Just for me.

Should I go home?

But what about the bagels?

If I went home, would I get bagels?

All I knew about was bagels.

Soft bagels. Sweet bagels. Freshly baked bagels.

I thought about the door to the yard.

I thought about the poster.

I thought about them calling "Cooeee Shnipp!" for me.

But I also thought about bagels.

And I went on going with Bessie to sell
bagels.

Chapter Three

One day, something happened that changed everything.

I was in the Bagel Van and I went to sit in my favourite spot under the cupboard. It was a bit of a squeeze to get in.

Once I was in there, I heard Julie and
Lara and Sadie outside. You know what
they were doing? Buying bagels!

But you see, though I had squeezed under the cupboard, I was now so big, I couldn't get out. I was stuck. The more I tried, the more I was stuck. I heard Julie and Lara and Sadie thank Bessie the Bagel Lady for the bagels and go off . . . but there was nothing I could do about it. I couldn't get out and run to see them.

In the end, Bessie pulled me out, but it was too late to catch up with Julie and Lara and Sadie. They were gone.

This made me think.

And after I had done some serious thinking, I decided to do something very important. I said to myself, "Look, I can't go on like this. What with all that stuff about the door and the posters and the *Cooeee! Shnipp!*, I miss them."

"And I miss running round and round the yard. I miss playing ball in the park. I even miss the snickering. I am going to find Julie and Lara and Sadie."

This is what is called "being decisive". It means, making up your mind to do something and then doing it.

I'm not just a dog with a big nose. I know some big words too.

That night, when we got back from the market, just as Bessie the Bagel Lady opened the door of the van, I made a dash for it. I ran.

I ran and ran and ran . . . I didn't know where I was running to . . . all I knew was that I had to get back to Julie, Lara and Sadie . . .

But – oh no!
I was lost. I didn't know where I was going.

I walked round streets I had never seen before.

I walked round a park I had never seen before. It wasn't the Memorial Park.

I walked round some more streets I had
never seen before.

I was completely and totally lost.

Chapter Four

Yes, once again, I was lost, but I wasn't thinking about the foxes. You never know when you'll run into a fox.

Right there, next to some huge wheelie bins, were some foxes. That's what happens when you're out and about. You meet foxes.

I dashed up to them, and I said, "Hey, guys, don't worry, I'm not after your eggshells. You're welcome to them. I'm not after your newspapers. You can keep them. I want to go home. Do you know Julie and Lara and their mum?"

And the others laughed . . . well, they snickered, actually.

"Not so lucky now, eh?" said one of them.

"Look," I said, "just show me. Please.
Can you show me the way to my old
house?"

So these foxes led me off down the road, round a few corners, along a few more roads, and there it was, there was the house . . . but . . .

. . . the door to the yard was shut. There was no way in.

I can tell you straight: this was upsetting.
This was very, very, very sad.

Let's have a sad moment while we all think about how sad I felt.

Even the foxes thought it was sad. They put their heads down and went off slowly, leaving me there on my own.

But . . .
and this
is a very
big BUT.
In fact it's
a huge
BUT.

As I stood there in the street outside the house, I could hear a growling sound. It was a dog. It was coming from the other side of the garden wall. I realised that Julie and Lara and Sadie had got another dog!

What?!!!!!
Another dog?!!!!!
How dare they?!!!!!

Chapter Five

I was furious. I was so angry. How could they? *I, Shnipp, am their dog,* I thought.

And just then, I heard Sadie calling for
this . . . this . . . this *dog-thing*, in the same
way as she used to call me . . .

Sadie should've been saying "Coooeeee! Shnipp!" Not "Coooeeee! Fotz!"

OK, yes, I know I've been gone a long time, I thought. *But why did you give up on me?*

Hmmm, well, yes, maybe if I was Julie, Lara or Sadie, waiting for their pet to turn up, I would have given up too.

Even so, I was cross.

So I stood on the other side of the garden wall and I growled too. Believe me, I growled. That was just about the biggest growling in the universe.

It was so big, that I heard the back door open, and I heard Sadie come out of the house and into the yard and say, "Don't worry, Fotz, dearest little darling, it's only foxes. They're just after some old eggshells, or something."

But Fotz went on growling and so did I.

Sadie opened the garden door and there I was.

There she was.

There Fotz was.

There Julie was.

There Lara was.

That's a lot of there-was-ing.

Sadie grabbed me and gave me the biggest hug there ever was.

Then Julie grabbed me and gave me the biggest hug there ever was.

Then Lara grabbed me and gave me the biggest hug there ever was.

That was a lot of ever-was-ing.

And now for the really, really, really difficult bit:

Now there was me AND Fotz.

And we were doing some very serious growling now. Growling for our lives. With my growl I was saying, "It's me or Fotz. Not both."

With his growl, Fotz was saying, "I live here now, and you don't."

I can tell you, for the rest of that day,
we got through some big growling.
Huge.

Massive.

Not only that day.

That week.

That month.

Chapter Six

But, you know, you can't growl for ever. You might want to remember that:

You Can't Growl For Ever.

Julie, Lara and Sadie were very nice to both of us.

I had my salad and paella.

Fotz had his baked beans and egg sandwiches.

In the end it didn't seem as if there was much point in being horrible to each other any more.

One day Fotz said to me, "Oy yoy yoy, I've got a sore throat!"

"*You've* got a sore throat?" I said. "You
don't know what a sore throat *is*!"

"I can tell you," Fotz said, "you talking about your sore throat is giving *me* a sore throat."

"That's the trouble," I said, "here's me trying to tell you how sore *my* throat is, and all you can do is tell me about *your* sore throat . . ."

After a few hours talking like that, we decided to stop growling:

I said to Fotz, "Your growls sound more like breathing."

Fotz said to me, "Your growls sound more like breathing too."

"That's because my voice is going."

"Going?" said Fotz. "Where?"

"It's not going anywhere," I said. "I mean it's not working any more."

"Yes," said Fotz, "I know what you mean. Shall we stop doing the growling, then?"

"Yes," I said, "let's do that."

Then I had a thought.

"Hey," I said, "do you like eggshells?"

"No! Why would I?" asked Fotz.

"Well, do you like newspapers?" I said.

"No! I'll tell you what I really like . . ." said Fotz.

". . . BAGELS!" we both shouted. And now there was no need to growl, because we both agreed on bagels.

That's another big one: if you stop growling, you find you can get along.

One more thing. I know what you're thinking:

"What about the snickering?"

Look, in the end, even the snickering is no big deal, is it? I mean, people can laugh how they like, can't they? If people want to laugh so that it sounds like sneezing backwards, that's OK, isn't it? There are worse things in the world than people laughing in some way you or I might not like, don't you think?

And that's the end of my story.

A dog's story.

Shnipp's story.

Well, OK, it's Shnipp and Fotz's story.

One last thing:

Remember, you can't growl for ever.

Don't Forget Tiggs!

BY MICHAEL ROSEN
ILLUSTRATED BY TONY ROSS

Mr and Mrs Hurry are always rushing about. They never stop! But that means they sometimes forget some rather important things – like eating … and shopping … and taking their son Harry to school!

Thankfully, Tiggs the cat is around to remind them. But will anyone remember to give Tiggs his dinner?

'Funny family adventure. Brilliant for emerging readers'
The Bookseller

9781783442690   £5.99